The Pop Star Pirates

By Maggie Pearson

Illustrated by Dan Chernett

W
FRANKLIN WATTS
LONDON•SYDNEY

CHAPTER 1
The Three Runaways

This is the story of three bold pirates:

One-eyed Jake, Blackbeard and Peg-leg Pete.

They ran away from home because their

mothers made them help around

the house…and wash every day…

and never let them play loud music!

They found a hidden cove where they could laze around. They could swim in the sea, so they didn't need to wash.

They could play their music as loud as they liked: Blackbeard on keyboard, Jake on guitar...and Pete on the drums, using his peg leg as an extra drumstick!

They built a pirate ship out of planks of wood and old car tyres and empty barrels. Every night they dreamed of sailing the seven seas and having adventures and stealing loads of treasure.

Every day they lazed around...

...and swam in the sea...

...and played their music.

6

People could hear them far away.

But no one knew where the music was

coming from. No one discovered their

secret hide-out, until one day a little

boat rowed into the cove.

CHAPTER 2
The Visitor

"Ship ahoy!" cried Jake. "We've got a visitor."

"That's nice," said Pete.

"This is our secret hide-out!" said Blackbeard.

"We don't want visitors."

"We could just say hello," said Pete.

"Then ask them nicely to go away,"

said Jake.

"But we're pirates!" cried Blackbeard.
"What are we?"

"We're pirates," the other two mumbled.

"Pirates don't ask nicely. We have to scare them away!"

"What if we can't scare them?"

"Then we fight them!" Blackbeard jumped aboard the pirate ship.

"Hoist the Jolly Roger! All hands on deck! Prepare for battle! Cast off!"

But the pirate ship had got used to wallowing
in the shallow water with its bottom resting
on the warm, soft sand.

"Push!" yelled Blackbeard.

"We are pushing," puffed Pete.

"Push harder!" shouted Blackbeard.

"Why don't you come down and push?"
said Jake. All three of them managed to
push the pirate ship off the sand. Together
they jumped aboard and started paddling.

With two pirates paddling on one side and only one on the other, the ship kept trying to go round in circles. The little boat bobbed up and down as if it was laughing at them.

"I don't think this is going to work," said

Jake. "We're not going to scare them away."

"Then we'll have to attack!" said

Blackbeard. "As soon as we come alongside,

I'll say the word."

"What word?" said Jake.

"Jump!" said Blackbeard. "Here we go.

After three: One, two, three – jump!"

Together they jumped. The little boat rocked.

"Sit down!" said Bonnie-Ann.

The pirates sat.

"Welcome aboard," said Bonnie-Ann.

"Are you pirates?"

"We are!" said Blackbeard. "And this is our cove – our secret hide-out."

"Does that mean you want me to go?"

"Er – yes."

"Right, then. I'll go, just as soon as you get off my boat," said Bonnie-Ann.

"Right then," said Blackbeard. "We're going now."

But the pirate ship had drifted away while they were talking and was heading for the open sea.

"It looks like you'll have to swim," said Bonnie-Ann. "Or you can join my crew if you want. I've always wanted to be a pirate."

Now there were four bold pirates, lazing all

day on their sandy beach...

...swimming in the sea...

...and playing loud music. Jake on guitar,

Blackbeard on keyboard, Pete on the drums...

...and Bonnie-Ann singing, very loudly. She knew all the old pirate songs. Songs like *Fifteen Men on the Dead Man's Chest, What Shall We Do with the Drunken Sailor?* and *A Life on the Ocean Wave.* She could even dance the *hornpipe.*

The boys played while Bonnie-Ann danced. She didn't just dance. She pranced. She twirled and tapped. She hopped and skipped and jumped so high it was almost as if she was flying.

"She's amazing!" said Pete.

"Fantastic!" said Jake.

Blackbeard said nothing. He was too busy trying to keep up on the keyboard.

CHAPTER 3
Pirate Bootcamp

"You're not real pirates," said Bonnie-Ann

one day.

"We are real pirates!" said Blackbeard.

"You're not."

"We are!"

"Real pirates don't laze around all day," said Bonnie-Ann. "Real pirates have adventures. They sail the seven seas, fight battles and steal treasure. Real pirates have to be fit."

"We are fit!" said Blackbeard.

"Show me!" said Bonnie-Ann. "Let's see what you can do."

"Why don't we try running? Race you to the top of the cliff!" Bonnie-Ann won easily, partly because she got to the path first, so it was a bit like racing up a ladder. Mostly it was because the other pirates were tired out.

Every day after that, Bonnie-Ann
turned up with more get-fit exercises
for them to do.

She made them run up the cliff path carrying heavy rocks, pretending they were cannon balls to load the cannon up on deck.

"We haven't got a cannon," said Pete.

"And the boat's only got one deck," said Jake.

"We can pretend!" said Bonnie-Ann.

She made them swing on a rope across a crocodile pool. There were no crocodiles, but the pool was very, very muddy.

They spent hours hacking a path through the jungle, which turned out to be mostly brambles and nettles.

"We won't always be attacking from the sea," said Bonnie-Ann.

One morning they found a whole obstacle course set up.

"Where did she get that from?" said Jake.

"Search me," said Pete.

"She's Bonnie-Ann," sighed Blackbeard.

"What Bonnie-Ann wants, Bonnie-Ann gets," said Jake.

"I'm fed up with being a pirate," grumbled Pete, who'd got his peg leg stuck in the climbing net.

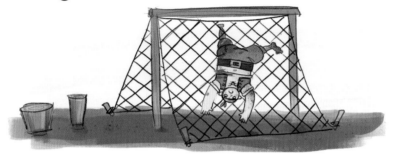

"I'm fed up with Bonnie-Ann," mumbled One-eyed Jake, who was lost under the tarpaulin.

help

"She's worse than my mum," sighed Blackbeard.

But next day Bonnie-Ann turned up with a treasure map! Maybe things weren't so bad after all.

" 'X' marks the spot," she said. "Off you go. Have fun!"

"Treasure?" said Pete.

"Real treasure?" said Jake.

"What are we waiting for?" cried Blackbeard. "Let's go!"

Off they went, following the treasure map...

up the cliff path and through the bushes...

down onto the next beach and over the

sand-dunes...then across the rocks and

round the headland, splashing through

pools that often turned out to be deeper

than they looked!

Blackbeard's beard got tangled in the brambles. Pete's peg leg kept tripping him up. Jake couldn't see on one side because of his eye-patch. He kept bumping into things.

But on they went, following the treasure map...until they found themselves back in their secret cove.

There was Bonnie-Ann, waiting for them.

There was a big X drawn in the sand.

"Start digging," she said, handing them

each a spade.

The pirates started digging. They dug

and they dug, but they didn't find

any treasure.

"Where is it?" said Jake.

"Where's what?" said Bonnie-Ann

"The treasure, of course," said Pete.

"There isn't any yet, silly," said Bonnie-Ann.

"This is where we're going to hide it when we've stolen it. See you tomorrow!"

CHAPTER 4
Mutiny!

"Why do we always do what Bonnie-Ann says?" growled Blackbeard.

"She's the captain," said Pete.

"It's her boat," said Jake.

"That doesn't mean she has to be captain," said Blackbeard. "Pirates used to vote for their captain. It could be anyone."

"Why didn't you tell us that before?"
said Pete.

"I was the captain," said Blackbeard.

"Who's going to tell Bonnie-Ann?" said Jake.

"We'll all tell her," said Blackbeard.

"She won't listen," said Pete.

"We'll make her listen," said Blackbeard.

Next day they lay in wait for Bonnie-Ann.

They jumped on her and tied her up.

"We're fed up with you being captain," said Blackbeard.

"OK. So who's going to be captain now?" said Bonnie-Ann.

"Me!" said Blackbeard.

"Me!" said Jake.

"Me!" said Pete.

"So it's a draw," said Bonnie-Ann.

"Do I get a vote? I am still one of the crew. Now, who shall I vote for? I suppose that depends on who unties me."

"I'll do it!" said Jake.

"No, let me!" said Pete.

"Out of my way," roared Blackbeard.

"Now who are you going to vote for?" they demanded.

"Me, of course," said Bonnie-Ann. "This is the day we become real pirates."

CHAPTER 5
Pop Star Pirates

Slow and stately, the pleasure steamer,

Skylark, sailed past the mouth of the pirates'

cove, just as it did every Saturday.

This Saturday was different.

"Ship ahoy!" cried the mate.

"Where?" said the captain.

"There!" said the mate. "It looks like there's been a ship wreck."

"Stop the engines! Man the lifeboat!" roared the captain.

"Look unwell," whispered Bonnie-Ann to the pirates crouching in the bottom of the little boat. "We're shipwrecked sailors. When they rescue us, say 'water, water'!"

"Water, water!" mumbled the pirates as the *Skylark's* crew helped them aboard the lifeboat.

"Water, water!" they mumbled again as they came aboard the ship.

"Water?" said the mate. "You must be sick of water. How about a smoothie? Or a milkshake? I expect you're hungry too. This way to the dining room. Help yourselves!"

Later on, Pete said, "I'm full."

"Me too," said Jake.

"We're not really going to rob anyone, are we?" said Blackbeard.

Bonnie-Ann sighed. 'I suppose not," she said. "But we could have done. My plan would have worked. That's what counts, isn't it?"

They were alone in the dining room.

"Where is everyone?" whispered Pete.

"Where have they all gone?"

"Perhaps it's a ghost ship," said Bonnie-Ann.

"That would be an adventure, wouldn't it?"

"I can hear music," said Blackbeard. "Do ghosts play music?"

"There's only one way to find out," said Bonnie-Ann. "Let's go and see!"

Softly the music swept through the ship…
upstairs and downstairs, whispering round
corners. The pirates followed it, creeping on
tiptoe – in case it did turn out to be ghosts –
till they came to a door marked 'Ballroom'.

The band looked bored. The dancers looked
bored. The people watching them looked
even more bored.

The pirates began to feel bored, just watching them. Then Bonnie-Ann said, "I've just had a great idea. Come on!" "We'd better go with her," sighed Blackbeard. "She's still the captain." Together the pirates marched up to the band. "We're pirates!" cried Bonnie-Ann. "This is a hijack."

"Can you hear music?" asked the captain.

"I can," said the mate. "It's very loud music. Someone's singing, too. Very loudly."

"We'd better go and see what's happening."

They followed the music through the ship until they came to the ballroom.

Pom Pom Pom Pom

There they found Jake playing the piano, Blackbeard on the guitar, and Peg-leg Pete on the drums. Everyone else was dancing the *hornpipe*, led by Bonnie-Ann.

"Why didn't you tell us you were a band?" said the captain.

"What do you call yourselves?"

"We're The Pop Star Pirates!"

"That's funny," said the mate. "When we rescued you, I said to myself, they look like a band of pirates. I hope this isn't a hijack!"

"Shall we dance?" said the captain.

"Why not?" said the mate.

"This reminds me of the old days," said the captain, "when I was sailing the seven seas in search of adventure. Every night we used to play loud music and dance the *hornpipe*."

"This is just what the *Skylark* needs," said the mate. Finally something to liven up these Saturday afternoon trips – thanks to The Pop Star Pirates!"

Now you have to book in advance for a place on the *Skylark* when she sets sail on a Saturday morning. There are four pop star pirates aboard.Three of them play loud music. One of them sings. You can hear them a long way away.

Tiddle Om Pom Pom

They always finish with the *hornpipe,* and Bonnie-Ann leads the dancing.

First published in 2014 by
Franklin Watts
338 Euston Road
London
NW1 3BH

Franklin Watts Australia
Level 17/207 Kent Street
Sydney
NSW 2000

Text © Maggie Pearson 2014
Illustration © Dan Chernett 2014

The rights of Maggie Pearson to be
identified as the author and Dan Chernett as
the illustrator of this Work have been
asserted in accordance with the Copyright,
Designs and Patents Act, 1988.

Series Editor: Melanie Palmer
Series Advisor: Catherine Glavina
Series Designer: Cathryn Gilbert

A CIP catalogue record for this book is
available from the British Library.

ISBN 978 1 4451 3357 7 (hbk)
ISBN 978 1 4451 3358 4 (pbk)
ISBN 978 1 4451 3359 1 (ebook)
ISBN 978 1 4451 3360 7 (library ebook)

Printed in China

Franklin Watts is a division of Hachette
Children's Books, an Hachette UK company.
www.hachette.co.uk